TABLE OF CONTENTS

Table of Contents 1

Learn how to balance life 4

Be Alone 5

Do not be afraid of failure 6

Think big 6

Establish a routine 6

Find what you love to do and do it 7

Make every minute of your life count 7

Do not be afraid of failure 8

Be a person of Action 8

Schedule everything 9

Cultivate positive relationships 9

Get enough sleep 10

Dare to introduce new ideas 10

Believe in your capacity to succeed 10

Take risks.. 10

Always maintain a positive mental attitude.................................. 11

Go big or go home..11

Don't let discouragement stop you.. 11

Prioritize..12

Be willing to work hard.. 12

Honour the code of responsibility.. 13

Be grateful.. 13

Final thoughts 14

Be prepared to learn... 14

Don't be afraid of having big goals.. 15

Focus on your strengths and passions, not your weaknesses 16

Think positive thoughts.. 16

Don't be afraid of having a big goal.. 17

Get rid of distraction.. 17

Plan, plan and plan again.. 18

Switch it up to avoid burnout... 19

Make a real commitment to success.. 20

Become a per sonic action.. 21

Don't be afraid of failure... 22

Stop looking for your straight bullet.. 22

Prioritize your physical health... 23

Talk to others.. 24

Take a break.. 25

Always be learning 26

HOW TO BE SUCCESSFUL IN LIFE

There are several books on how to be successful, yet success is personal and unique to each person. So how would the same information from each book be applicable to all? As a result, accepting a single person's advice is frequently ineffective.

With this in mind, taking the advice of a large number of individuals, people whose definitions of success differed from one another and, quite perhaps, from you, can be a great starting point.

Learn How to Balance Life

People frequently believe that in order to be successful, they must make the aim of their success their life. If people believe that their employment will lead to success, they may put in endless hours every day, often late into the evening.

However, this comes at the expense of relaxation, health, and enjoyment of life. They may eventually burn out and stop being effective in their career.

If their success is based on having a robust social life and a nice group of friends, their employment may suffer, and they may lose their job, leaving them unable to go out with friends.

As Knight mentions, balance aids achievement in numerous ways. Consider it a delicate balance of relaxation, labor, or work and enjoyment.

Be Alone

Make time for yourself. Turn off the TV, step away from the computer, and put down the phone. Embrace your "me time" and think about what made you happy today. Or, do not think at all. That's the beauty of being alone. The choice is yours.

Do Not Be Afraid of Failure

There's a narrative, and while it's unclear whether it truly happened, the message is still valid in understanding how to be successful:

Numerous fruitless attempts led to Thomas Edison creating the lightbulb. "How do you feel after all of your unsuccessful attempts?" he was asked in an interview.

"I didn't fail; I learned hundreds of ways not to develop the lightbulb," he said.

Each "failure" was a lesson to him. He learned what won't work and what may work instead from that lesson.

Every unsuccessful attempt was a crucial step on his journey to achievement. After a failure, it's easy to feel like you should quit, but perhaps it would be wise to find a teaching in that failure.

Some people associate success with money, others with power, and some from having a beneficial effect on the world.

They are all correct. Success has diverse meanings for different individuals. To you, it would mean one thing, while to others, it would mean something else.

There are several books on how to be successful, yet success is personal and unique to each person. So how would the same information from each book be applicable to all? As a result, accepting a single person's advice is frequently ineffective.

With this in mind, taking the advice of a large number of individuals, people whose definitions of success differed from one another and, quite perhaps, from you, can be a great starting point.

Think Big

His art continues to inspire and connect people decades after his death. Think what would have happened if he had decided not to pursue a career as an artist. Would he have ever found out how to become successful?

People frequently opt to put their aspirations on hold in favor of something more "practical." To forego their dream in favor of something simpler. Be ambitious instead.

Establish a Routine

Try waking up at the same time each morning. Enjoy breakfast and plan your day. Instead of feeling stressed or frazzled, find comfort in knowing you can control some things in your life. When you have your bearings, it's easier to take on new challenges and kinks in the system.

Find What You Love to Do and Do It

This is an excellent quotation to remember and reflect on at work when you are trying to find out how to be successful.

Consider how successful you could be in your current position. In the end, you'll probably find yourself working incredibly hard and devoting a significant amount of time to it.

Make Every Minute of Your Life Count!

If you dislike your job, being successful at it can just mean filling your life with things you despise. What is the point of this?

Why not do something you enjoy? You gain the motivation to keep advancing after you've discovered what you're enthusiastic about. Your aspirations will come true if you succeed in this.

Still undecided about your passion? You should first become acquainted with your Motivation Engine.

To discover your own Motivation Engine, join Lifehack's free Fast-Track Class – Activate Your Motivation. In this intense session, you'll delve deep into your inner drive and passion and create your own Motivation Engine based on it, ensuring that you never lose motivation again, even when things become rough.

Even if you weren't successful, you spent your time doing something you enjoyed. Many successful artists spent years of their life performing for free, and the only reason they continued to play was that they enjoyed it.

Do Not Be Afraid of Failure

There's a narrative, and while it's unclear whether it truly happened, the message is still valid in understanding how to be successful:

Numerous fruitless attempts led to Thomas Edison creating the lightbulb. "How do you feel after all of your unsuccessful attempts?" he was asked in an interview.

"I didn't fail; I learned hundreds of ways not to develop the lightbulb," he said.

Each "failure" was a lesson to him. He learned what won't work and what may work instead from that lesson.

Every unsuccessful attempt was a crucial step on his journey to achievement. After a failure, it's easy to feel like you should quit, but perhaps it would be wise to find a teaching in that failure.

Be a Person of Action

Even though it was spoken hundreds of years ago by Leonardo da Vinci, it still holds today.

Consider this: Consider someone like William Shakespeare:

When we think of the time he lived in, we think of it through his eyes. We think of Michelangelo and Leonardo da Vinci when we think of Renaissance Italy. Consider Bill Gates or Steve Jobs in the contemporary day. If they hadn't accomplished what they achieved, our contemporary way of life would be unimaginably different.

You're most likely viewing this article on a gadget made by a firm they either established or inspired.

These people were proactive; they identified opportunities to do things differently and took action. They shaped the world instead.

How does this apply to you when you try to learn how to achieve success?

Don't be frightened to deviate from the standard if you want to learn how to be successful. If you can develop a better method to accomplish anything, go for it. Try again if you fail.

Schedule Everything

Scheduling means keeping to a set time and not deviating from what should be accomplished. Successful people know there is no room to delay what has to be done now. They are realistic about the meeting, and they keep to their schedules.

Successful people know that procrastination is one of the biggest disruptors of a productive day. Instead of putting things off, try making a list of all the things you want to get done in a day. Checking things off will give you a sense of accomplishment and help you visualize the time you'll need for everything else.

Cultivate Positive Relationships

The finest leaders and some of the most important individuals in history were always nice to those around them.

They were well received. They wished for them to succeed. This is key to good leadership.

It makes sense.

You never know who will be someone who can assist you much or even be a terrific and supportive buddy. As a result, assist others, and they may assist you, be kind to others, and be kind to you.

Get Enough Sleep

Successful people know that they need to get adequate rest to get the best out of their performance. The body needs to be recharged and reactivated to get going for the next day's work. They do not deter themselves from the needed rest, which will get them re-energized.

It's important to know what can stand in the way of a good night's sleep. Using electronics while lying in bed, eating foods high in sugar before sleeping, or maintaining high-stress levels throughout the day can all get in the way of a good night's sleep. Take care of these before settling in for the night.

Dare to Introduce New Ideas

Unfortunately, people with the most daring ideas are sometimes overlooked.

From a young age, most of us are trained to think and act the same way as everyone else. However, you must think differently to do things differently (as all great individuals did).

If you get a novel thought, appreciate it instead of discarding it because it is novel and unusual. Your weird new concept might be the key to your success one day.

Believe in Your Capacity to Succeed

You must be able to visualize yourself reaching success if you wish to understand how to be successful.

Walt Disney was living proof of that.

You'll probably encounter those who question your abilities to achieve. You must not become one of these individuals because your dreams will vanish if you stop believing and dreaming.

Keep dreaming!

Take Risks

Don't be afraid to get your feet wet and try new things if you want to find out how to be successful at work. Think to yourself, "what is the worst that can happen?" For example, maybe you are not a fan of seafood. Your friend offers you sushi, but you are afraid to try it. Maybe this sushi is covered with fresh strawberries and lemon poppy seed glaze over white tuna. You love strawberries.

How would you know you hated sushi if you didn't try it? What's the worst that can happen? You spit it out. Life is about risks. You'll never know until you try.

Always Maintain a Positive Mental Attitude

As stated in the quotation above, you must have faith in your potential to achieve. This is the only way to develop a positive mentality.

Negative ideas should be replaced with postive ones. You must regard challenges as tasks to be done rather than as roadblocks to your progress.

Setbacks won't bother you as much, people's doubts won't bother you, and even the toughest barriers will seem trivial if you keep optimistic and think like this.

It will be much simpler to stop if you have the wrong mentality of doubt.

Go Big or Go Home

Embrace your talents and strengths, and go beyond what is required. If you need to turn in a paper for your boss by Friday, have it edited, reviewed, and submitted on Thursday. Try a new recipe and commit if you want to bake for a picnic. If you want to land that big promotion, work hard and prove that you deserve it.

Aspire to be successful, and you will not fail. Maybe you won't meet your goal or win, but you tried. You showed gumption, which is a great feeling that cannot be duplicated.

Don’t Let Discouragement Stop You

It’s an unpleasant aspect of human nature that we all doubt ourselves somehow. This might be exacerbated if others share our doubts.

Giving up might seem like a decent choice when uncertainties surround you. Pay no heed to your doubts. If you’re feeling down, ignore it.

Prioritize

Successful people focus on being excellent at what they do. Multitasking has its ills and can down your work performance. Knowing that multitasking often gets in the way of productivity, successful people prioritize and eliminate what will not gear them towards their success.

Be Willing to Work Hard

You may have heard the phrase “success is 1% inspiration, 99 percent perspiration,” or you may be familiar with the 10,000-hour rule.

Whatever way you look at it, they all say the same thing: Work is the key to true success.

If you don’t strive for your life objective and maintain working at it, you’ll never be successfula quote by the founder of jc penney inc.

you may have heard the phrase “success is 1% inspiration, 99 percent perspiration,” or you may be familiar with the 10,000-hour rule.

whatever way you look at it, they all say the same thing: work is the key to true success.

if you don’t strive for your life objective and maintain working at it, you’ll never be successful

Honor the Code of Responsibility

We want to know it all and have it all. On the contrary, we have the principle that you have a responsibility to everyone and responsibility for only yourself. Your life is multi-faceted.

See how you can contribute to your community. Join a volunteer group, participate in a charity, or help someone in need.

Follow Your IntuDelphi was the home of a set of Oracles in ancient Greece. From the lowest of society to rulers, everyone who sought counsel or wanted to know their destiny came to them. The words "know oneself" were written over the temple's gateway.

If you truly believe and desire something, you almost certainly already know how to get there. If not, you may instinctively know what will assist you and hinder you.

It's similar to how your body may sense danger even when things appear to be safe.

If you want to know how to be successful, you must trust your own intuition.

Be Grateful

If you want to know how to be successful, learn to be connected to others. Successful people boost their self-esteem and self-worth by appreciating the people around them. They can thank you and show appreciation for anything good they have received. Doing this helps their confidence and activates their brain to enjoy and make the best use of their environment.

Being grateful can be tough during hard times. To get started, try working with a gratitude journal. Every evening, write down three or more good things that happened during the day. This will help your brain get oriented toward the good and away from all the downers of the day.

Final Thoughts

You may have noticed that many of the preceding lessons are similar in that they all focus on cultivating the correct mindset. This obviously indicates that the key to success in whatever endeavor you pursue is the mental approach you use.

Think positive thoughts

One of the first steps towards success is to rid yourself of negativity.

We've all heard the phrase "you are what you eat," but a more accurate expression may well be "you are what you think."

If you focus on negative thoughts, you're unlikely to ever achieve success or happiness in life. But if you're positive and motivated, you can do anything.

Consider babies for a moment. When a baby learns to walk, they won't achieve their goal immediately. They'll fall and fall and fall again. But the important thing isn't the failing; it's the determination to get up and try again no matter how hard it seems.

We can learn a lot about determination and positive thinking from babies. Instead of constantly thinking "I can't," try thinking "I will." This simple exercise will allow you to feel more positive and motivated to achieve your goals, even when things feel impossible.

Remember what Gautama Buddha said: "Your mind is a powerful thing. When you fill it with positive thoughts, your life will start to change."

Be prepared to learn

As Colin Powell said, "there are no secrets to success. It is the result of preparation, hard work, and learning from failure" that defines us. But the minute you stop being willing to learn new things is the minute you leave the path to success behind.

Take time to notice and learn new things every day. Even if you consider yourself to be an expert on a subject, you'll be amazed to discover all the things you never realized you didn't already know.

But being prepared to learn new things can go so much further than simple facts or stories. Be prepared to learn how to deal with disappointment, how to prevent burnout, and how to celebrate your victories along the way. Every day provides a chance to grow and learn. Successful people know this and take full advantage of it.

Don't be afraid of having big goals.

There are countless books and guidance resources that claim the best way to become successful is to set yourself small, achievable goals to tick off as you go. But many of these people are afraid to think big.

Thinking big doesn't mean you shouldn't have a plan and smaller steps, but it does mean that you have a dream and a goal that you can work towards.

So many people put aside their big dreams to work towards something more "realistic" or achievable. But successful people don't care how ambitious their dreams might appear to others. All they know is that it's what they really want and that they're not afraid to go for it.

Think positive thoughts

One of the first steps towards success is to rid yourself of negativity.

We've all heard the phrase "you are what you eat," but a more accurate expression may well be "you are what you think."

If you focus on negative thoughts, you're unlikely to ever achieve success or happiness in life. But if you're positive and motivated, you can do anything.

Consider babies for a moment. When a baby learns to walk, they won't achieve their goal immediately. They'll fall and fall and fall again. But the important thing isn't the failing; it's the determination to get up and try again no matter how hard it seems.

We can learn a lot about determination and positive thinking from babies. Instead of constantly thinking "I can't," try thinking "I will." This simple exercise will allow you to feel more positive and motivated to achieve your goals, even when things feel impossible.

Remember what Gautama Buddha said: "Your mind is a powerful thing. When you fill it with positive thoughts, your life will start to change."

Don't be afraid of having big goals.

There are countless books and guidance resources that claim the best way to become successful is to set yourself small, achievable goals to tick off as you go. But many of these people are afraid to think big.

Thinking big doesn't mean you shouldn't have a plan and smaller steps, but it does mean that you have a dream and a goal that you can work towards.

So many people put aside their big dreams to work towards something more "realistic" or achievable. But successful people don't care how ambitious their dreams might appear to others. All they know is that it's what they really want and that they're not afraid to go for it.

Focus on your strengths and passions, not your weaknesses

So often in life, we spend our time focused on improving our weaknesses and just take our strengths for granted. This isn't the best way to become successful, or happy for that matter.

Instead of spending all your time and effort working on the things you're not good at or not passionate about, focus on the things you are good at. Not only to help you decide what your goals in life should be (we've already established there's no clear-cut answer to that one) but to help you see what skills you have that will help you along the way.

And it's important not to stop there. Just like there are always new things to learn, there are always ways you can improve your skills and change your life. Successful people are never satisfied with just being "good" at something. They want to be the best and will put all their effort into it.

And while you're at it, try to keep track of the things that make you happy and that you enjoy doing. Particularly when success is based on your career, you know you'll be spending a decent chunk of your life working at it. So it's vital to find something that makes you feel fulfilled in body and soul, as well as in your bank account!

Like Steve Jobs said – "Your work is going to fill a large part of your life, and the only way to be truly satisfied is to do what you believe is great work. And the only way to do great work is to love what you do."

Fostering a mindset that passion = success is the best method of achieving success. And chances are, the thing you love is already the thing you're pretty good at!

Get rid of distractions.

Let's face it, no matter how badly you want to make yourself successful, when there's a show on Netflix you're desperate to watch, your phone keeps pinging, you just know something exciting is happening on Instagram, it's all too easy to focus on things that aren't helping you achieve your goals.

That's why it's vital to get rid of excess distractions and negative thoughts on the path to success.

Now, that doesn't mean you can never binge-watch a series again… But it does mean that you need to focus up and commit real time and attention to your goals.

For example, if your goal is to start your own online business; while you work, your phone should be on silent or in another room if you can't be trusted not to look at it. If your dreams involve spending more quality time with your children, don't waste the moments you have checking work emails or watching sports.

If you want a successful life, you need to be prepared to work for it. And this might mean sacrificing short-term pleasures for future gains.

Successful people know that the difference between achieving success and simply experiencing disappointment and frustration along the way really comes down to whether you allow distractions to interrupt your life. Or whether you cultivate good habits that will help your dreams progress.

If you're not sure what's getting in the way of your success, pay attention to the things you're doing and thinking about daily. Are these things helpful to you? Or, are they just preventing you from knuckling down and working hard?

If it's the second one, you know it's gotta go!

Plan, plan, and plan again.

If you're serious about being successful, you need a plan in place to help you achieve your goals. And yes, this should be a big plan. A big huge goal that reflects your wildest dreams, and you can work towards it every day.

But a dream-big mindset will only get you so far. You also need to keep track of your progress towards a successful life. And to do this, you'll need a detailed plan that sets out how, when, and what you're going to do on the journey.

For example, if you want to have a certain amount of money by the time you reach a particular age, you need to know how you're going to achieve it. This includes whether you'll continue working with your current company, try your skills in a new career, or get a side hustle or learn how to make money online.

You should also make a plan for when you're going to do these things. Maybe you decide you want a new career and become your own boss, but you're not willing to take the plunge just yet. In that case, make a plan to leave your employment in a certain length of time and stick to it. If you want more money but are happy with your job, decide when you'll ask for a pay rise. And stick to it.

Many people talk about success but struggle to keep track of their progress, challenges, and habits that are helpful/unhelpful to their goals. But you'll only ever achieve success with a detailed plan that you stick to, no matter what.

Switch it up to avoid burnout

When you're highly motivated to succeed in life and have a strict plan to track your progress, it can be easy to get caught up in the mindset that only your goals matter. But this is a mistake.

The most successful people know that self-care and taking time out are also vital for ensuring success in life. Only focusing on your career, money, or other goals to the exclusion of anything else that provides you with joy will only lead to burnout and dissatisfaction.

Not only is taking time for yourself vital for your mental health, but it's also the best way to ensure you're in tip-top condition to actually achieve your dreams. Without rest, your mind and body can't recover, and you'll soon find that you're not working at 100%.

Therefore, if you genuinely want to be successful, take time to do things that aren't part of your plan too. Whether it's meditation, breathing exercises, or a trip to the waterpark... Give yourself permission to practice mindfulness and even have fun once in a while!

And if you are experiencing burnout or you feel lost for ideas... Taking time out can help too. Don't waste your time sitting at a blank computer screen. Get up, stretch, maybe go for a walk or call a friend. When you come back, you'll feel better and are sure to be more productive than if you'd sat and struggled.

Make a real commitment to success.

Many people think you need to be motivated to be successful. But this isn't entirely true. When you commit to yourself (or others), you'll likely find that the motivation will come if you give it a chance.

Just because you don't feel motivated to write that best-selling novel you've always talked about doesn't mean you shouldn't try. If you're committed to writing, the words will come, and the motivation will grow as you see yourself moving closer to the finish line.

It's important to remember that not every day will be easy as you work towards success. You will make mistakes. You will face challenges. And you will have days where you simply don't believe you'll ever make it.

But if you're committed and keep trying, successful life is possible.

If you're not great at self-motivating, there's also no harm in asking others to help you maintain your commitment and dedication to your goals. This could be as simple as asking your friends not to invite you out so you can spend time with your family or having someone help you build a budget to better manage your money.

Although nobody can achieve success for you, they can absolutely help you on your journey and ensure you stay accountable.

Become a per sonof action

One of Walt Disney's most famous quotes is "the best way to get started is to quit talking and start doing," along with "all our dreams can come true, if we have the courage to pursue them."

While these might sound a little corny, we can't help but see Walt's point: you'll never achieve success if you're not willing to take the first step towards it.

If you really want success in life, you can't just talk about it. All the plans in the world are useless if you don't take action and take the first step.

And we get it; there's always a reason not to take a risk. Whether you don't want kids because you're worried it will affect your chances of a promotion or you're scared to quit your secure job and focus on your dream of owning a business... There will never be that perfect moment to start this journey. So stop waiting.

The trick to success is to take the plunge anyway and keep trying even when it gets tough, or you're afraid you might make a mistake. The only mistake is not to try.

Don't be afraid of failure.

No matter how talented, motivated, committed, passionate you are or how much you want to learn and succeed, failure is an inevitable part of every journey and one you'll have to deal with throughout your life.

However, it's vital to learn that failure doesn't always mean the end of the road. It just means you need to try a different path or put in some extra practice before achieving your goals.

So many people decide not to take a risk because they believe they will fail. But "the greatest failure is not to try" (Debbi Fields). And you'll always regret a missed opportunity if fear of failure stops you from taking the first step.

And if fear of failure really is stopping you from living your dreams, we recommend you consider this quote from Barack Obama: "The real test is not whether you avoid this failure, because you won't. It's whether you let it harden or shame you into inaction, or whether you learn from it; whether you choose to persevere."

As Obama wisely said, failure is inevitable. But choosing to give up or keep going is down to you. And it may well make you stronger, wiser, or better in the meantime.

Stop looking for your silver bullet

No matter how many social media adverts claim that you can make thousands of dollars overnight, or self-help books promise to revolutionize your life... The simple answer to how to be successful is that there is no simple answer.

The key to success isn't a pill or a hack or a conference. It's not being afraid of failure, learning from mistakes, and believing in yourself. It's showing up and trying again and again until you get it right.

So, think about what it is you really want to do. Make a goal, then make a plan for how you will achieve that goal, and stick to it. Over time, you'll develop habits and a mindset that will help you overcome any challenges, so you can be successful in life... No matter what that means to you.

Prioritize Your Physical Health

It is easy to get caught up in the never-ending wheel of tasks we need to accomplish each day and checking off items from our to-do list.

But, if you want to find success, it is important to make your physical health a priority. Being physically fit and healthy makes you feel better about yourself so you can think more positively. It also literally makes you feel energized physically and capable of accomplishing more things.

Some of the most successful people have attributed being health conscious as one of the keys to being successful in life. Highly successful people prioritize both their physical and mental health.

Make sure you eat healthy foods and minimize unhealthy foods and drinks. Develop an exercise routine that includes physical activity each day. Get plenty of rest to rejuvenate your mind and body, which will help you be more productive when it is time to work.

Believe In Yourself And Your Abilities

If believing in yourself doesn't come naturally, make a list of all of the positive attributes you have.

Are you organized? A good listener? Do you make excellent pumpkin pies, do you hold productive team meetings or do you make people feel good about themselves? Are you great at generating ideas, or does your strength lie in taking those ideas and making a plan of action.

One of the best ways you can be successful is to learn how to believe in yourself and boost your self-confidence. Greater self-confidence motivates you and gives you the courage to take action on your goals.

When you feel discouraged, focus on what you have accomplished and the time, talents, abilities, and strengths you have that will help you accomplish more.

When you believe in your abilities to achieve your goals, you have the power to persevere until you succeed.

Have Fun!

We can easily get overwhelmed by the craziness of life and stress over things that need to be done.

In order to have a successful life, you need to be happy. And one of the best methods for happiness is fun.

Purposefully find a ray of fun in every day. See the humor in a stressful situation and laugh about it to diffuse tension. Studies show that even simply putting a smile on your face lowers your blood pressure and heart rate when things are stressful.

Get out and play, devote time to a hobby you love, watch a funny video and develop a good sense of humor.

Talk To Others

Having someone to bounce ideas off of, talk to and hear feedback from about how you're portraying yourself to others can be extremely helpful when building yourself to be successful.

Look to those you trust and respect for feedback, like close friends and family members. Although everyone will have an opinion on how you are conducting your life, the opinions that matter are from those who have your best interest at heart.

It may be difficult at first to receive constructive criticism. But do not let it deflate you but uplift you instead. The opportunity to change for the better is a gift that makes a lasting impact on your current and future happiness.

To find success in life, you must continually grow. Talking to others you trust about how you make improvements can make a substantial difference in your progress.

Take A Break

Burnout can happen fast if you keep chasing your goals without taking a rest.

Taking periodic breaks will have a positive impact on your progress toward your goals.

To find success in life, it's actually beneficial to spend time away from your goals to reset and recharge. Your goals will still be there even after a day or even a week off for your mental health.

Be careful not to wait until you are at the end of your rope before taking a break. An essential part of recharging is the small breaks you take throughout your day and week to keep your life balanced.

If a particular task or situation is causing frustration, step away from it for a few minutes. Get your mind off of it by doing or thinking about something completely different. Coming back to it with renewed eyes and perspective will help you accomplish it faster and with greater effectiveness.

Always Be Learning

Try learning one new thing every day — whether in your personal or professional life.

We grow as we learn, so in order to succeed, prioritize learning as much as you can on a daily basis.

When you dedicate your time to becoming a lifelong learner, you're sure to find success in life. A lifelong learner takes initiative to continue learning and improve personal development.

When you are always learning, you improve your quality of life and are exposed to more opportunities that can lead to fulfillment and satisfaction.

www.ingramcontent.com/pod-product-compliance
Lightning Source LLC
LaVergne TN
LVHW080600160826
845677LV00010B/1930
* 9 7 9 8 8 4 8 3 3 6 7 1 9 *